To Santino Ray with love - H.O.

First published in Great Britain in 2013 by Andersen Press Ltd.,
20 Vauxhall Bridge Road, London SW1V 2SA.
Published in Australia by Random House Australia Pty.,
Level 3, 100 Pacific Highway, North Sydney, NSW 2060.
Text copyright © Hiawyn Oram, 2013.
Illustration copyright © Satoshi Kitamura, 2013.
Printed and bound in Malaysia by Tien Wah Press.
10   9   8   7   6   5   4   3   2   1

British Library Cataloguing in Publication Data available.

ISBN 978 1 84939 625 7 (hardback)
ISBN 978 1 78344 042 9 (paperback)

Beetle and Bug and the Grissel Hunt

Written by
Hiawyn Oram

Illustrated by
Satoshi Kitamura

ANDERSEN PRESS

Beetle and Bug had a magic rug
Which went if they gave it a pull and a tug
It could fly through the air; it could swim through the sea
So wherever they told it to go, there they'd be.

"The ocean!" said Bug. "Where we haven't yet been
On the hunt for something that's never been seen
Like the Green-Spotted Grissel, the finding of which
Will make us incredibly famous and rich."

"Well, we'd better take flippers and lots of fresh air,"
Said Beetle, "I'm told that there isn't much there."
So they boarded their rug and they gave it a jerk
And set off to find Grissel where Grissel might lurk.

They looked through the weeds and swam through the shoals
They searched every reef and examined the holes
They rummaged round rocks, every crevice and crack
Every lump in the sand, every watery track.

"There!" Beetle yelled. "That flash of bright red
Tucked up and asleep in the oysters' bed . . ."
"Or there," gurgled Bug, "in the trail of that whale,
I'm willing to bet that's a Grissel's tail."

So they went up close and they saw what they saw
Which was nothing they'd seen in their lives before.
An enormous belly with bright green spots
All covered in scales and small purple dots,

With billowing bumps and bulges and lumps
And bobbles and blisters and nobbles and humps
Attached to a tail full of hundreds of hoops
And tangles and wiggles and squiggly loops.

"It must be a Grissel," said Beetle, "for sure,
It's like nothing we've seen in our lives before
And it does have a body all smothered in dots
And it's certainly covered in bright green spots.

And it has got a tail full of hundreds of hoops
And terribly Grisselly wiggles and loops
And there . . . at the end . . . at the tip . . . there's a fork!"
"Then that's not a Grissel," said Bug. "IT'S A MAWK!"

Well, they weren't after Mawk so they left those seas
And turned their thoughts to the galaxies.
"Since space," said Bug, "is more likely the place
To meet up with a Grissel . . . more face to face."

Then stopping just once for something to wear
Like boots and some suits and a lot more air,
They flew on their rug at a reckless pace
To hunt for a Grissel in empty space.

They looked through the dust, the craters and bowls
They rummaged round rocks and searched all the holes.
They peered round at nothing and stared through the void
Till Beetle cried . . . "THERE! ON THAT ASTEROID!"

So they went up close and they saw what they saw
Which was nothing they'd seen in their lives before.
All covered in needles and prickles and spines,
In some very peculiar curves and lines

It was huge and jelliferous – jelly with hair
And some of its parts were less round than square
Its paws had great claws while its head was so small
You needed your specs to see it at all.

"It must be a Grissel," said Beetle, "for sure,
It's nothing we've seen in our lives before
And it does have peculiar curves and lines
And terribly Grissel-like prickles and spines."

"But it hasn't a tail," said Bug, "or good dots
And it certainly hasn't got bright green spots
And a Grissel's not meant to be big as a bus

AND WATCH OUT, BEETLE,
        IT'S COMING FOR US!"

So they left that Alien-being in space
And boarded their rug for a friendlier place.
"Home!" cried Beetle. "And it's great to be back
Let's put Rug to bed and look for a snack!"

So they searched through cupboards and rummaged in bins
They examined the oven and looked in the tins
They opened the freezer – though there wasn't much there
But a few trays of ice and a lot of cold air . . .

Then they went to the fridge and saw what they saw
Which was nothing they'd seen in their lives before,
For smacking its chops with a grunt and a grind
Was the last thing on earth they wanted to find . . .

"It's a G-NUZZLER!" said Bug. "It must be for sure
You can tell by its G-Nuzzelly teeth and its jaw."
"And the way that it's licking," said Beetle, "that bowl
That once held a wonderful Toad-in-the-Hole,

And the way that it's scoffing those bangers and mash
And munching that honey-roast ham and that hash
Not to mention that hotpot, that haggis, that tripe
Those peaches and plums that were just getting ripe."

Then the G-Nuzzler said, "Hmmm, what you say is quite true,
I'm a G-Nuzzler for sure and what about you?
But do close that door as I really can't bear
Being hit while I dine by a blast of hot air."

So they closed the fridge door and they went off to bed
Without any supper – not a nibble of bread
Where Beetle said, "Bug, we have been into space
And down in the ocean, all over the place.

We have seen a Great Mawk and a Spine-Covered Bus
And a G-Nuzzler, who guzzles what should be for us,
But no Spotted Grissel, the finding of which
Might make us incredibly famous and rich.

Now if you ask me, and on this I insist,
It will never be found as it doesn't exist.
So though being famous and rich would be sweet,
Tomorrow we're hunting for "SOMETHING TO EAT!"

Then they said, "Goodnight, Rug," settled down with a sigh
And dreamed the night long of gooseberry pie.